ly Pets

BIRDS

EZ READERS

Miriam Z.

Creating Young Nonfiction Readers

EZ Readers lets children delve into nonfiction at beginning reading levels. Young readers are introduced to new concepts, facts, ideas, and vocabulary.

Tips for Reading Nonfiction with Beginning Readers

Talk about Nonfiction

Begin by explaining that nonfiction books give us information that is true. The book will be organized around a specific topic or idea, and we may learn new facts through reading.

Look at the Parts

Most nonfiction books have helpful features. Our *EZ Readers* include a Table of Contents, an index, a picture glossary and color photographs. Share the purpose of these features with your reader.

Table of Contents

Located at the front of a book, the Table of Contents displays a list of the big ideas within the book and where to find them.

Index

An index is an alphabetical list of topics and the page numbers where they are found.

Picture Glossary

Located at the back of the book, a picture glossary contains key words/phrases that are related to the topic.

Photos/Charts

A lot of information can be found by "reading" the charts and photos found within nonfiction text. Help your reader learn more about the different ways information can be displayed.

With a little help and guidance about reading nonfiction, you can feel good about introducing a young reader to the world of *EZ Readers* nonfiction books.

Printing 1 2 3 4 5 6 7 8 9

Author: Miriam Z.
Designer: Cornell Whitehead
Editor: Editorial Staff

Names/credits:
Title: Birds / by Miriam Z.
Description: Hallandale, FL : Mitchell Lane Publishers, [2018

Series: Pets Books

Library bound ISBN: 9781680202076

eBook ISBN: 9781680202083

EZ readers is an imprint of Mitchell Lane Publishers

Photo credits: Getty Images

Table of Contents

Birds.......................................4
Parts of a Bird..........................22
Picture Glossary 23
Index.......................................24

I want a pet bird.

Which one
should I get?

Birds come in all sizes and colors.

Birds sleep in a cage.

I have to
clean the cage.

Birds eat seeds and drink water.

They fly around.

Some even like to sing.

A pet bird can be a good friend.

Parts of a Bird

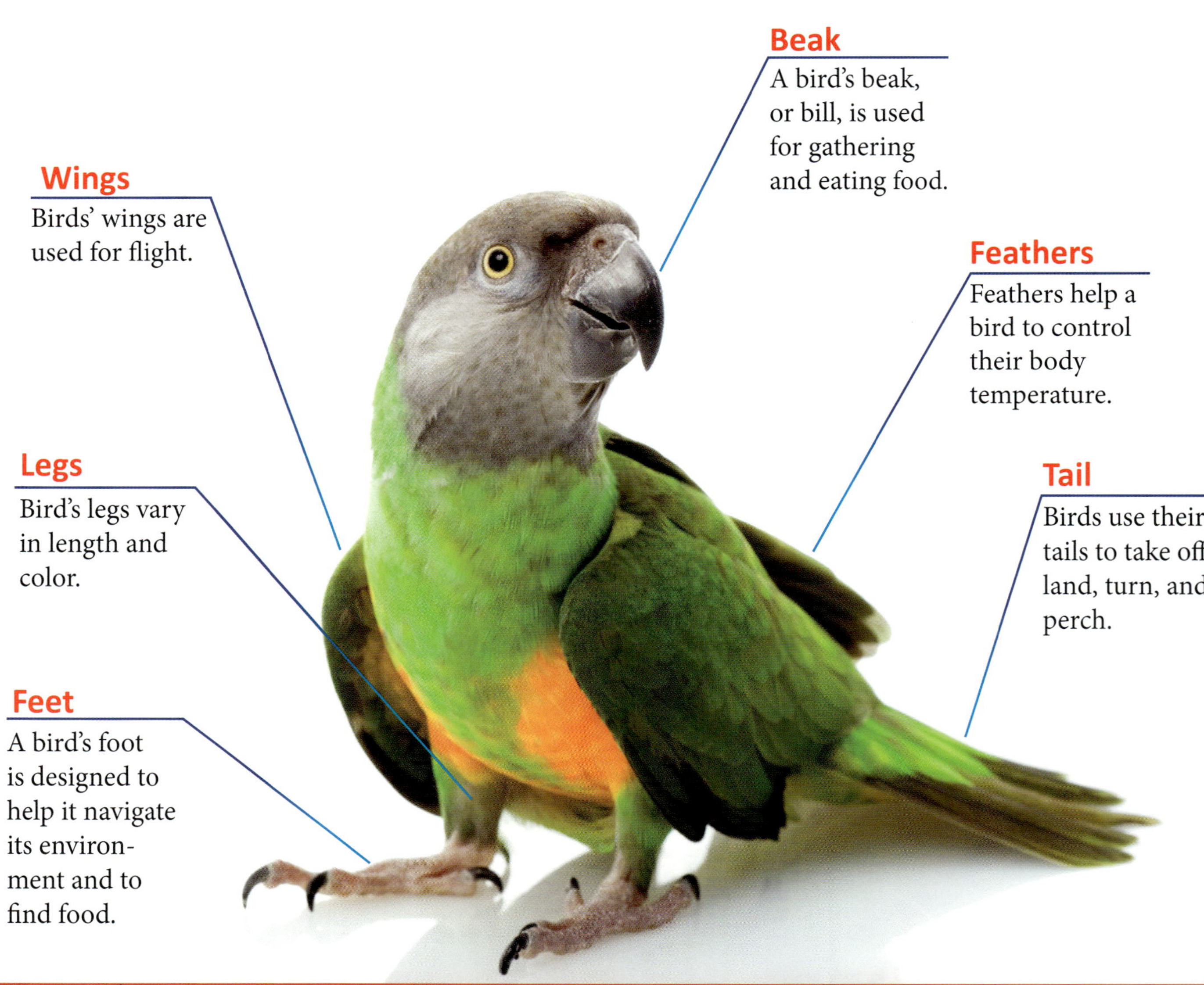

Picture Glossary

cage

A box made of wire or metal bars in which people keep animals.

seeds

An object produced by a plant from which a new plant can grow.

clean

To remove dirt, marks, etc., from something.

sleep

To rest your mind and body.

friend

Someone who is your pal or companion.

Index

cage 10, 13
clean 13
colors 8
fly 17
friend 20
seeds 14
sing 18
sizes 8
sleep 10